"Sometimes you don't know what you want for Christmas until you see it." Frank hiked his thumb at Glosser's big display window. "Sometimes it's right in front of your face."

Frowning, Sarah peered into the window...and froze.

On the other side of the glass, a mechanical Santa Claus sat on a red wooden rocking chair, reading an enormous paper scroll that could only be his nice/naughty list. The part of the scroll he'd finished, the part that flopped over his red-mittened hand and was readable to Sarah, wasn't what she would have expected. Another scroll of paper had been laid over the list, inscribed with a message in big black letters.

"ELF SARAH," read the message. "YOU ARE INVITED TO ATTEND GLOSSER'S CHRISTMAS PARTY WITH SANTA CLAUS!"

Sarah stared for a long moment, stunned. Frank had caught her off-guard.

"Like it?" Frank rapped on the glass, and the faces of two male employees popped out from behind the green background curtains. "The guys in the display department set it up for me."

Sarah's head was spinning. She had hoped to keep pretending a while longer, but she was going to have to tell him. She was going to have to own up about Mike.

She had a fiancé in the service overseas, and she couldn't break her promise to marry him when he got back.

Or could she?

A Glosser's Christmas Love Story

By Robert Jeschonek

pie press publishing

DEDICATION

To the men and women of Glosser Bros.,
who brought such passion to everything they
did, especially during the holidays.

Johnstown, 2016

Even before Jason kissed her, Emma thought it was a perfect moment.

Snowflakes fluttered down around them, drifting lazily out of the night sky. The cold air was barely moving, only lightly stirring her long black hair. Strings of white lights clung to the spindly tree branches around them, giving off a magical glow.

Best of all, the giant Christmas tree in the middle of Johnstown's Central Park danced with colorful patterns of light, flashing and changing in time to the holiday music playing from nearby speakers.

Jason's face had been bathed in the blinking light from that tree when he pulled her close. "I'm so happy when I'm with you." His cheeks had flashed red and green when he'd said those words. "I mean, *every* time I'm with you."

Emma's heart had been pounding. She could have sworn it had been beating in time with the song that was playing--"Let it Snow."

"I feel the same way," she'd said. "It's like we were made for each other."

Smiling warmly, he'd reached out and traced the line of her jaw with the tip of his finger. "You're the greatest Christmas gift I've ever gotten in my entire life." Breath misting in the cold December air, he'd leaned closer. "I love you, Emma."

That was when their lips had met, after he'd said those words for the first time.

For that one perfect moment, Emma felt transported. The wintertime city of Johnstown, Pennsylvania melted away around her, leaving her suspended in another realm of perfect warmth and happiness. All she could feel were Jason's lips pressed against hers...Jason's arms wrapped around her body...Jason's heartbeat through the coats they wore.

There were people around them (the tree drew big crowds for the holiday season) but Emma was blissfully unaware of any of them. Only the man who was kissing her seemed to be real. Only Jason Halloran seemed to matter.

It was like something out of a dream...

Only when the song changed to "White Christmas" did they break the kiss. Even then, they stayed close, with foreheads touching.

"I love you, too," she told him softly.

He kissed her again, longer this time. People around them were singing along with the music, which somehow made the second kiss more romantic than the first.

Emma knew she would never forget this night. It was the first time the two of them had said those words, announcing they loved each other. And it was the first time they'd been together during the holiday season. After all, they'd only met three weeks ago.

And in just a few days, they would spend their very first Christmas together. She could hardly wait.

But she also wanted to savor every magical moment, to enjoy it for all it was worth.

The music changed again, to "Rockin' Around the Christmas Tree." Jason broke the kiss...but again, did not pull away. "Want to get some hot chocolate or cider?"

Emma nodded. "Okay." Something hot to drink sounded like a good idea on a cold night.

The truth was, anything seemed like a great idea as long as he was with her. She had a good feeling about him, a *great* feeling, unlike any other boyfriend she'd ever known in the 27 years of her life so far.

It was a feeling that stayed with her as they left the big, flashing tree and headed for the lights of the busy Press Bistro up ahead, across the street on the corner of Locust and Franklin.

*****

The place was packed when they walked in, full of people in a festive mood. Ever since the tree had gone up, the Press had become one of the hottest places in town, especially on Saturday nights like this one.

At first, Emma thought they might not find a table... but an elderly couple sitting by one of the windows waved them over from across the crowded room.

"The table is all yours." The man, who might have been in his seventies or eighties, pushed himself to his feet. "We were just leaving."

"That's very kind of you." Emma smiled. "We were just enjoying the tree."

"We know." The woman, who looked about the same age, grinned and nodded. "We saw you two canoodling out there."

Emma blushed. Jason laughed and kissed the top of her head.

"Young love at Christmastime." The old woman sighed as the man helped her up by the elbow. "It's good to see."

"Brings back memories," said the man. "Walking through the park in the old days, then looking at the holiday decorations in the windows--right here." He gestured at the window by the table. "Back when this was Glosser Bros. Department Store."

"It was a magical place during the holidays." The old woman nodded as the man helped her on with her heavy brown coat. "So many lovely decorations in the windows

4

and all through the store. People coming and going, buying presents. Christmas music playing, everyone feeling good."

"That's why we still love coming here so much," said the man. "Glosser's store is gone, but this restaurant brings back some of the same good spirits."

"My grandmother used to work here," said Emma. "At Glosser's."

The woman blinked from behind her thick glasses as she buttoned her coat. "What department, dear?"

"The grocery store and a few others," said Emma. "She always says how much she loved it here."

"Then you and your beau have certainly come to the perfect place tonight." The old woman smiled and patted Emma's arm. "The perfect place to get to know each other better."

With that, she and the old man said goodbye and worked their way through the crowd to the door. Emma and Jason sat down beside each other, holding hands.

"What a cute couple!" said Emma.

"Want to hear something crazy?" Jason squeezed her hand. "*My* grandfather used to work at Glosser's, too."

"For real?" Emma felt a thrill of excitement ripple through her.

"I know, right?" Jason smiled and shook his head. "What a coincidence."

"I wonder if they were here at the same time!"

"I wonder if they knew each other."

"I wonder." Emma loved the thought of another

connection between them, another link that seemed to confirm how meant-to-be they were. It was like the dream-come-true just kept getting better.

"We need to find out," said Jason.

"I'll have to talk to Gram," said Emma. "Ask her what she remembers. What's your grandfather's name?"

"Frank," said Jason. "Frank Halloran. What's your grandmother's name?"

"Sarah Jensen," said Emma. "She's my mom's mom."

"Cool. So I'll call my grandpa in Michigan and see what he says about Glosser's," said Jason. "And Sarah."

"I'll see her tomorrow," said Emma. "So I'll talk to her then."

"Awesome." Jason drew her hand up and kissed it. "Wouldn't it be cool if they knew each other back in the day?"

*****

It was snowing hard the next afternoon when Emma pulled up to the apartment building in Richland Township, the suburb of Johnstown where Sarah lived. At least the parking lot was mostly clear; someone had plowed it so the usual crowd of Sunday visitors would have plenty of open spaces to occupy.

Parking her ten-year-old blue Honda Civic at the edge of the lot, Emma walked around front and entered the vestibule. When she hit the button for Sarah's apartment, the inner door buzzed open, and she stepped through.

The big front lobby was overflowing with holiday decorations. There were fully decked trees in each of the four corners, each with a different color scheme and theme. Evergreen boughs entwined with red ribbons and colored lights ran along the chair rail on the wall and wrapped around the pillars in the corners. The big mahogany table in the middle of the room was covered with festively wrapped packages trimmed with gold and silver bows. Somewhere nearby--in the dining room, maybe--Christmas music played softly.

Emma winced at the sight and sound of it all. She could only imagine how much her grandma hated it.

As far back as she could remember, for reasons she never knew, her grandmother had always hated Christmas.

Passing through the lobby, Emma swung right and headed down the hallway, which was also strung with boughs, ribbons, and colored lights. Every door was decorated, too--covered in wrapping paper, ribbons, and bows like gift-wrapped presents.

As Emma walked, she smelled something baking, though she couldn't quite figure out where it was happening. She got her answer when she followed the bend to the one door that wasn't gift-wrapped--number 116, her grandma's place. The baking smell was coming from there, no question.

When Sarah opened the door--before Emma could knock, as always--the smell rushed out and engulfed her.

There was nothing like it in the world, nothing better (except, perhaps, the smell of Jason's cheek). It instantly made her think of childhood and Sunday dinners at Gram and Grandpap's big old house on Highland Avenue in Moxham.

Sarah ambushed her with a hug the second her toe crossed the threshold into the apartment. "Emmy Lou!" She always called Emma that, though her middle name wasn't Lou. "Get your coat off and come help me with these cookies!"

"Only if I can have one first!" Emma's eyes widened when she saw the racks of cooling chocolate chip cookies in the little kitchen behind the door. Was there anything more delicious than warm cookies straight off the rack?

Warm cookies baked by *Gram? So what* if they were distinctly un-Christmaslike, in keeping with Gram's rejection of anything associated with the holiday.

"Coat first, hon." Sarah, 86 years old and barely five feet tall, was still a bossy, brassy individual. "And wash those hands! Twenty seconds and plenty of soap!"

"Yes, ma'am." As Emma stripped off her black-trimmed bright red coat, she looked around the little apartment. As with every Christmas season, there wasn't a holiday decoration anywhere to be seen--no tree, no boughs, no ornaments, not even a card set up on a table. It was like Christmas wasn't even happening, as far as Gram and her apartment were concerned.

In years past, at least, Grandpap Mike had put up a few

decorations in keeping with tradition. But things weren't the same with him gone, and the old house sold, and twelve years passed since things had stopped being the way they used to be. There was no one else who could convince Sarah to put up a sprig of holly or a Christmas stocking.

After washing her hands in the bathroom, Emma returned to the kitchen and snagged a cookie. "Mmmm." It was every bit as melty and delicious as she'd expected. "Thank you, Gram, thank you."

"Mm-hm." Sarah straightened her apron--which was more like a sleeveless housecoat, white with red plaid hip pockets and a blue back--and handed over a spatula. "Now less eating, more working, sweetheart. We've got another batch coming out of the oven in..." She glanced at the old egg timer on the counter. "...one minute."

Emma automatically started stacking the cookies on a plate on the counter. "Say, Gram. Back when you worked at Glosser's, did you know a guy named Frank Halloran?"

"A guy named what?" Sarah was a little hard of hearing sometimes.

Emma spoke up. "Frank Halloran. Jason's grandfather. He moved to Michigan ages ago, but he lived in town and worked at Glosser's. Did you know him?"

Suddenly, Sarah froze. She just stood there and stared into space.

"Gram?" Frowning, Emma stopped plating cookies and took a step toward her. "Gram, are you all right?"

"I haven't heard that name in ages." Sarah's voice

was hushed. Her fingers clutched the silver locket that she always wore around her neck. "Frank Halloran."

Just then, the timer dinged. The cookies in the oven were done.

"Who is he, Gram?" asked Emma.

Sarah's eyes glittered when she met Emma's gaze. "The love of my life," she said. "And we met at *Glosser's.*"

*****

Johnstown, 1953

"You dropped something." The young man with the bright green eyes and red hair held up a 20-lb. frozen turkey and grinned. "Here you go."

Sarah Jensen stopped in the frozen food aisle of the Glosser Bros. grocery store and shook her head. "Not *my* turkey, thanks."

"But it is!" The guy pushed the frozen turkey toward her. "I clearly saw it fall out of the pocket of your sweater."

Sarah shrugged and sighed. She wasn't in the mood to goof around that morning, not after the letter she'd gotten before coming to work. "You must be confusing me with someone else."

"Not a chance." The guy's smile turned charming. "There's *no way* I could ever confuse you with anyone else."

The smile made Sarah hesitate. She was 23 years old,

after all, and he was...he was...

Not completely unattractive. His eyes were bright as emeralds, his hair red as firelight. He was six feet tall, with a slim, athletic build and muscular shoulders. And he was about her age or a little younger, perhaps a little older.

But no. She had her reasons for not socializing these days. And besides... "I need to get back to my register," she told him. "My lunch break is over."

"So?" He lowered the turkey, revealing the Glosser Bros. nametag pinned to the chest of his white button-down shirt. "I'm not even *on* break."

The tag, stamped with the name "Frank," caught Sarah off guard. She hadn't known he was a fellow employee. She'd never even seen him before he shoved the turkey in her face.

Not that it made any difference. "Look, I really have to get back to my register," she said.

"Then what am I supposed to do with *this?*" He turned the turkey over in his hands, looking forlorn.

It was then she was seized by the inexplicable impulse to throw him a bone. "Put it in the oven for six and a half hours at 325°," she said. "Either that, or roll it down the aisle and use it to bowl for customers."

"Brilliant!" Frank perked up. "You're a genius..." He peered at the nametag pinned to Sarah's gray sweater. "...you *Sarah*, you."

"That's what they tell me." Sarah smirked. "I'm a genius, all right."

As she started to walk away, Frank stepped in front of her. "See you around?" He smiled expectantly.

"I guess so." Reaching up, she pushed a lock of her chestnut brown hair behind her right ear. "Though I've never seen you around before today."

"That's because this is my first day on the job." He winked. "But you'll be seeing me a lot more from now on."

"Is that so?" Sarah looked toward the checkouts in the front of the store. If she didn't get back to her post soon, someone would come looking for her.

"Absolutely." Frank nodded enthusiastically. "I'm like a bad penny. I keep turning up."

Sarah shrugged and headed for the checkouts. Frank backed away and disappeared in the frozen food department.

Up front, she returned to her register, apologizing for being late to the girl who'd been covering for her. The girl, a chatty redhead, didn't seem to care as she stepped away from the checkout and Sarah replaced her.

As the next customer put her items on the counter, Sarah punched their prices into the register. She slid cans of corn and green beans into the bagging area at the end of the counter, and someone caught them.

At first, Sarah didn't look to see who was doing the bagging. But as she finished ringing everything up, she turned...and there he was.

Frank Halloran himself grinned back at her as he loaded the items into big brown paper bags.

Sarah just stared. She hadn't expected to see him there.

"Ma'am?" Frank was talking to the customer. "Shall I carry these upstairs for you?" Offering to haul purchases was expected, since the grocery store was located in the basement of Glosser's department store. It was a long walk up and out to the parking lot or on-street parking, especially with a heavy load of groceries.

"Yes, please." The customer, a heavyset middle-aged woman in a pale green coat and squat cream hat, nodded. "My car is out back in the lot." With that, she paid Sarah, got her receipt, and briskly started toward the nearby flight of stairs to the first floor.

Frank followed with a bag in each arm. He winked at Sarah as he followed the customer, mouthing four words that made her smile in spite of herself.

Penny for your thoughts?

*****

Frank wasn't kidding about the bad penny stuff. He worked as a bagger at her checkout every day. When she went on break, he showed up beside her at the lunch counter in Glosser's cafeteria. When she left at the end of the day, he walked out with her.

And soon enough, he started hinting around about going out with her. She brushed it off, pretending she didn't hear him...but she knew she couldn't keep playing dumb forever. Sooner or later, she had to tell him the truth.

She had to tell him exactly why there could never be anything between them.

Though the truth was, she didn't really mind the attention. It was nice for a change, even though he was a little too persistent. It had been too long since anyone but Mike had acted that way with her, and Mike...

Mike wasn't around. He'd been overseas for two years.

But Sarah knew she had to put her cards on the table at some point. If only Frank wasn't *there* so much, and wasn't so *nice*...maybe it would be easier. If only he didn't make her *laugh* so much. If only...

Then, one morning, she got her wish. Billy Cruikshank, not Frank, stepped up to bag groceries at her checkout stand.

"Where's Frank?" she asked.

Billy shrugged. "Dunno." As usual, he had a blank look on his face. A tubby, swarthy guy in his thirties with a crewcut, he had a reputation for not being "all there" since returning from fighting in Korea.

Talking to him made Sarah's heart sink, and she quickly turned away. Now that Frank wasn't there, she instantly missed him.

And hated herself for feeling that way.

*****

Later, Sarah sat down at her usual spot at the lunch

counter in Glosser's cafeteria and pulled out a pack of Lucky Strike cigarettes. She was just about to light one when the place erupted into chaos.

"Ho ho ho!" A man dressed as Santa Claus burst into the room, shouting to the high heavens. "Who's been *naughty*, and who's been *nice*?"

"Nice!" hollered the Shaffer twins, Ruth and Ruby, from behind the counter.

"Naughty!" shouted sassy Mary Schuster from the adjacent Hunt Room restaurant.

Howling with laughter, Santa grabbed a gift-wrapped present out of his sack. Bells on his sleeve jingled as he waved it overhead. "Today, *everyone* gets a present, naughty *or* nice!"

"Got any hooch in there, Santa?" asked Mary--known as Hunt Room Mary to her customers and colleagues.

"Open your present and see!" Santa tossed the wrapped gift her way, and she caught it. "Better hope it's not a lump of coal!"

"I'll kick your fat behind if it is!" said Mary.

"Ho ho ho!" Santa handed gifts to Ruth and Ruby, then made his way around the counter to Sarah. "And what about you, young lady? Naughty or nice?"

Before Sarah could answer, he pulled a small box wrapped in silver paper out of his sack. "Wait! I already know!" He bowed at the waist as he handed the gift to Sarah with a flick of his wrist, sleeve bells jingling. "You're *always* on the nice list, aren't you?"

Smiling, Sarah took the package and undid the red ribbon crossed around it. With one fingernail, she broke the single piece of adhesive tape sealing the paper. Then, she slowly unwound the silver paper from the box.

Frowning, she studied the cubical Glosser Bros. box underneath. It sat in the palm of her hand, big enough for some kind of jewelry...or whatever little surprise Santa might have in store for her.

"Go ahead and open it, Sarah." Santa pointed a red-gloved finger at the box and winked. "Don't you want to see what Santa brought you?"

It was the wink that gave him away. Finally, Sarah saw through his disguise and realized who was under the beard and costume.

And she froze. She couldn't bring herself to open the box.

"C'mon, honey!" shouted Hunt Room Mary. "Show us what Santa brought you!" She pulled a green and red plaid sweater out of her gift box and shook it with glee. "Just look what *I* got!"

"Yeah, Sarah!" said Ruby. "Let's see it!"

"Let's see it!" said Ruth.

Still, Sarah hesitated. Since that was Frank in that Santa Claus costume, she could only imagine the gift he might have brought her.

She had a pretty good idea how he felt about her, after all. And the box in her hand was the exact size commonly used for gifts of jewelry.

And jewelry was something she could *not* accept from *him*.

"I can't." She tried to give the box back to Frank. "I really can't."

He wouldn't take it. "I insist. You've been very nice lately, and you deserve this gift."

Sarah shook her head. "No, really." She put the box down on the counter. "I have to get back to work."

"You've really lost it, haven't you, sweetie?" said Hunt Room Mary.

"Santa Claus always knows best!" Frank grabbed the box, tipped the lid open, and held it out for Sarah to look inside. "See what I mean?"

She did...and how.

Her eyes flew wide open, and a huge smile flashed onto her face. She let out a little yelp of delight and quickly flung her hands over her mouth as if to keep any more yelps from escaping.

"What?" Ruth and Ruby said it simultaneously as they crowded in from behind the counter.

"What the heck is it?" snapped Hunt Room Mary.

Sarah giggled and reached into the box. "It's the best gift ever!" She pulled out the object resting on the cotton padding inside and held it up to watch it glint in the bright cafeteria light.

"Huh?" said Ruth and Ruby.

Hunt Room Mary hustled over and squinted at what Sarah was holding. "Well that is one cheap gift, if you ask me. Santa Claus can be a real *skinflint*."

"But it's not just *any* penny," said Sarah.

"It's a *bad* one," said Frank. "The kind that keeps turning up! Ho ho ho!"

It was then, in that moment, that Sarah had the urge to hug him. Because the truth was, she had been so very lonely for such a long time...and she cared for him, and she liked the way he treated her.

And the way he made her laugh.

So she did it. She went ahead and hugged him.

And she made a decision. She wasn't going to talk about Mike, not with Frank. At least for a little while.

*****

After her shift that afternoon, Sarah spent some time shopping in the store upstairs, searching for gifts. She did all her shopping at Glosser Bros., since she got to use her employee discount to save money on purchases.

She'd had her eye on a thing or two for Mom, and she knew it was time to buy. With just a few days until Christmas, the place would be completely picked over soon.

As it was, Glosser's was packed with shoppers, grabbing items off tables and racks. Twice, Sarah got elbowed by women in the accessories department...but she didn't mind. Holiday music was playing, and decorations hung everywhere. The smell of fresh chocolates and roasting chestnuts filled the air.

Even with all the heartache in her life, Christmas at Glosser's was her favorite time of year.

"Your mother is going to *love* these." Margie the sales clerk draped the pretty white kid gloves in a gift box on the counter. "And that beautiful *hat* you picked out...! Such lovely gifts, Sarah!"

"Thank you." Sarah smiled. "I can't wait to see her open them."

Margie, a pretty brunette just a little older than Sarah, put the lid on the box of gloves. "There's a nightgown upstairs that I've had *my* eye on for a while." Smoothly, she pulled a piece of gift wrap out from under the counter and folded it around the box.

"Sounds perfect for your mother," said Sarah.

"Who said anything about *her*?" Margie cocked her head, looking dead serious...then laughed. "So how much more shopping do you have to do?"

"This is it." Sarah had already bought her dad a new lunch bucket and overalls. An only child, she didn't have any brothers, sisters, nieces, or nephews to buy for. "All done."

Margie stuck a bow on the box and handed it over. "So you've already bought something for your fiancé then?"

"Oh yes." Sarah had bought and shipped the gift over a month ago. It took a while to get to Korea, after all.

And it took even longer to get back, sometimes. That was what she'd read in the depressing letter the other day--that Mike, her fiancé, who'd already been gone two years, wasn't coming home for at least another six months.

The damn Korean War didn't seem to care what she felt. Though the truth was, these days, she wasn't so sure what she felt anyway. She didn't even wear her engagement ring to work anymore, though she said it was because it got in the way when she handled groceries and ran the cash register.

"Good for you." Margie punched buttons on the cash register, ringing up the sale. "Won't that be something when he finally comes home?"

"The best gift ever." The words came easy, but they felt hollow. Had Mike been gone too long? Had they lost whatever was special between them?

Or was it something else?

Just then, Sarah heard jingling bells from across the store. Instinctively, she looked in that direction, expecting to see Frank in his Santa Claus costume.

But this time, it was just a sales girl shaking jingle bells for a laugh. Sarah slumped.

"Why so disappointed?" Margie followed her gaze. "Did you think it was Santa?"

"No, no," lied Sarah.

"He *is* a handsome boy under that beard, isn't he?" Margie smiled, then dropped her voice to a whisper. "Do you think I should go sit on his knee and tell him what I want for Christmas?"

Sarah shrugged and pulled the change purse out of her pocketbook. "That's how it works, isn't it?"

"I suppose." Again, Margie spoke in a whisper. "I wonder if he'd bring a present down *my* chimney?" She giggled.

Sarah smiled as she paid for her purchases...but wasn't amused. For the first time, in fact, she felt something new toward Frank, something she hadn't expected.

She felt *jealous.*

*****

Sarah was working at her checkout the next day, ringing up a customer, when a conical deep green cap was suddenly thrust in front of her face.

"Quick! Put this on!"

Startled, Sarah quickly looked to see who was pushing the cap at her, even as her housewife customer's two small children called out his name.

"*Santa!*"

"That's right, kiddies!" Naturally, it was Frank in costume again. He spent all his working hours dressed as Santa Claus these days. "And this fine lady is my very special *helper* today!"

"I am?" said Sarah. "Says who?"

"Says Rudolph!" Frank winked at the kids--a little boy around 6 or 7 and a girl around 4 or 5--and they cheered again. "He said you're the best elf in all of Glosser's!"

Sarah didn't love the idea of dressing up like an elf. "Tell Rudolph I'm very busy here at my register today."

"Lucky you, Elf Sarah! Mr. Glosser himself gave you special permission to work with Santa for the day!" Again, Frank shoved the green cap in her direction.

"Which Mr. Glosser?" asked Sarah.

"*All* of them!" With that, Frank reached up and lightly placed the cap on her head. "You can come upstairs to the North Pole as soon as you finish ringing up this customer."

"Yes, please." The housewife customer sounded annoyed. "Finish ringing me up, please."

"Sorry, ma'am." Flustered, Sarah returned her full attention to the groceries and cash register. She punched in the prices of the few remaining items, announced the total cost, and got the correct amount of cash from the customer. No change necessary.

Meanwhile, Santa Frank took care of bagging the groceries, since Billy the bagger was away at the moment. The kids loved it and watched his every movement.

"Are you gonna carry our stuff up to our car?" the little girl asked excitedly.

"Ho ho ho! Of course I am!" said Frank. "As for *you*..." He grinned at Sarah as he scooped up the two bags of groceries. "I'll meet you at the North Pole when I get back."

Sarah was stuck and she knew it. If Mr. Glosser--*any* Mr. Glosser--had given the go-ahead, she had to play ball.

Taking off the elf cap, she turned it over in her hands, thinking how ridiculous it would make her look...and then she smiled. Frank was certainly full of surprises. And she had to admit, once again, that she was flattered by the attention. It was nice, even if it could never go anywhere. It was nice to make believe for a while, after being so lonely for so long.

Laughing to herself, she put the cap back on her head and switched off the light above her register, closing the checkout. She would give the elf business a try.

There were worse ways to spend an afternoon.

*****

"You want a *what?*" Santa Frank sounded stunned by what the little boy on his knee had said. "A *real* rocket ship?"

The kid, who couldn't have been older than six or seven, nodded so decisively, the red-and-black hunting cap with the giant brim and ear flaps flopped forward over his eyes.

Grinning, Sarah stepped up and raised the cap so it sat back on his head. She had to admit, she was having fun playing elf for the day.

"Can we even *do* that, Elf Sarah?" Frank asked her.

"Hmm." She pretended to think hard about it. "Rocket ships take a long time to build. What about a really neat *toy* rocket ship until we get the *real* one ready to go?"

"Ho ho ho!" Frank gave the kid a shake. "What do you say to that, sonny?"

The little boy thought it over, then nodded. "It's a

deal!" The hat flopped down again, and he pushed it back himself this time.

"Good for you! Now watch the birdie!" Frank pointed at the camera mounted on a tripod ten feet away, manned by an overweight middle-aged photographer in overstretched green tights and a cap like Sarah's. "Smile for Harry the Photo Elf."

"Dat's me." Harry, who usually manned the loading dock, peeked around the camera, looking like he'd rather be somewhere far away. "Say cheese, kid."

The kid said it, the camera flashed, and Frank helped him down off his knee. Sarah held out the basket of candy canes for him to take one...but the kid took three and ran off to rejoin his mother.

Before the next kid in the very long line could move in, Sarah stepped in front of Frank. "Do you want to take a break?"

"No, ma'am." Frank shook his head. "Keep 'em coming."

"But you haven't taken a break since we started," said Sarah.

"Maybe in a few minutes." Frank leaned forward and winked. "I love this, you know."

There was a twinkle in his eye when he said it. He really did make a great Santa Claus, Sarah realized.

It made her like him all the more.

"Well, you just let me know if you need anything," she said.

"As a matter of fact, I *do* have a question," said Frank. "What do *you* want for Christmas, Elf Sarah?"

She shook her head. For the longest time, she'd wanted one thing, but now she couldn't have it. If Mike wasn't coming home for Christmas, she couldn't think of anything else she really wanted.

Or maybe she *could*.

"What about you?" She turned the question around on Frank. "What do *you* want for Christmas, Santa Claus?"

"I already have it." His eyes locked with hers, and he smiled warmly behind his bushy white beard. "You don't even have to ask."

Sarah's heart raced. His gaze, his voice, his words-- the message was unmistakable. The feelings were there in him...but did she *share* them?

And what could she do if she did? She was *engaged* to another *man*.

Suddenly agitated, Sarah cleared her throat and spun to face the crowd waiting in line. "Who's next?"

"I am! I am!" shouted a sweet little girl with curly blonde hair and a black fur-trimmed coat.

"Santa will see you now." Sarah waved the girl forward.

"My name is Grace!" said the girl as she hopped up on Frank's knee. "I want a dolly and a milkshake!"

"What flavor?" asked Frank.

"Chocolate!" said Grace. "For the milkshake!"

Frank chuckled. "Have you been good this past year?"

"No." Grace shook her head. "The op'site."

"Well, at least you're honest." Frank patted her on the head and grinned at Sarah. "Santa likes honesty."

Sarah felt uncomfortable and looked away.

"Time for your picture, Grace." Frank pointed at the camera. "Smile nice for Harry the Photo Elf."

"Dat's me." Harry lit a cigarette off a match and peeked around the camera, looking bored.

"What about the *other* elf?" Grace pointed at Sarah. "Could she get in the picture, too?"

Frank laughed. "I don't see why not. Come on over here, Elf Sarah."

Sarah hesitated but wanted to make little Grace happy. She stepped behind the ornate throne on which Frank sat and leaned down to smile over his left shoulder.

"Say cheese," said Harry, puffing smoke from his cigarette.

It was then, with a bright flare of the camera's flash bulb, that he snapped the shot.

*****

Working as an elf could be exhausting. That was why, as Sarah trudged outside after her shift, she only wanted to go home.

Standing on the corner of Franklin and Locust streets, she pulled a cigarette out of her coat pocket and lit it. The tip glowed red as she drew the warm smoke into her lungs, relishing the taste of it.

Just then, as she prepared to head for the bus stop, she heard the door crash open behind her and a familiar voice call her name.

"Elf Sarah!" It was Frank. "Need a lift?"

"No thanks." Sarah was still a little stung by his earlier comment about honesty. Did he know about Mike? Had someone told him? "See you tomorrow, though."

Frank--in a navy blue pea coat and watch cap instead of the Santa suit--looked crestfallen. But then he quickly shook it off and smiled. "May I walk you to the bus stop, at least?"

Sarah puffed on the cigarette and blew out some smoke. "Okay, sure." Maybe he'd clue her in about the honesty comment along the way.

They started down the walk along the Locust Street side of the Glosser Building, lit by the glowing display windows. Those windows were the showpieces of Glosser's, especially at Christmastime. People came from all over to see the elaborate holiday displays even if they didn't plan to actually shop at Glosser's.

"So that was a fun day today, wasn't it?" Frank walked between Sarah and the street, hands folded behind his back.

"It was." Sarah smiled as she remembered the parade of children who'd come to see Santa.

"I love making kids happy, don't you?" said Frank. "And Christmas is my favorite time of the year."

"Mine, too," said Sarah.

Frank drew a deep breath, then let it out. "It makes *me*

feel like a kid again." With that, he darted around behind her to look into the nearest display window. "I remember it like it was yesterday."

Sarah paused for a look, too. Inside the window, the figures of three happy children were posed around a grinning snowman wearing a top hat and corn cob pipe--Frosty himself, in the middle of a one-window winter wonderland.

"Now *that* is Christmas to me." Frank pressed his hands against the glass. "I used to stand here for ages and look in at those wonderful visions and *dream*."

"I've always loved these windows, too," said Sarah. "I look forward to them every year."

"People always make such a big deal about Penn Traffic's windows. Not me." Frank tapped his finger on the glass. "I was *always* a Glosser's fan."

Continuing on, he stopped at the next window and smiled. Sarah thought he looked handsome in the reddish glow from inside.

"Working here was a fantasy of mine when I was a kid," said Frank. "But getting to play *Santa Claus* is something I never imagined! It's the best ever!"

Stepping over beside him, Sarah gazed into the window. This time, the scene was right out of a typical living room on Christmas morning. There was a fully-decorated Christmas tree off to one side, and two little boys unwrapping gifts. Mother and father mannequins watched over them in bathrobes and slippers, holding presents of their own.

"I think I've finally found my calling." Frank reached under his pea coat and pulled out his red Santa hat with the white fur trim. "Forget the steel mill. I wanna be Santa Claus." Grinning, he pulled on the hat and posed for her with arms folded over his chest.

Sarah chuckled. Mike had never been this funny or surprising. In her time with him, she'd forgotten how much she missed it.

"So you never answered my question, Elf Sarah," said Frank. "What *do* you want for Christmas?"

"I really don't know." Sarah took one last puff on the cigarette, then dropped it to the sidewalk and crushed it out with the toe of her shoe. "Maybe I'm too old for that sort of thing."

"Never!" Frank jabbed an index finger overhead. "You are *never* too old for Christmas!"

Sarah shrugged. She didn't think he understood, and she didn't want to try to explain. "It's for children, anyway."

"There *has* to be something you'd like." Frank marched to the next window and stopped. "Maybe a little more window shopping will help?"

Sarah checked her watch. It was almost time to catch the bus.

"Sometimes you don't know what you want until you see it." Frank hiked his thumb at the window. "Sometimes it's right in front of your face."

Curious, Sarah walked over to stand beside him.

Frowning, she peered into the window...and froze.

On the other side of the glass, a mechanical Santa Claus sat on a red wooden rocking chair. As three pointy-eared elves looked on expectantly, Santa read an enormous paper scroll that could only be his nice/naughty list. But the part of the scroll he'd finished, the part that flopped over his red-mittened hand and was readable to Sarah, wasn't what she would have expected. Another scroll of paper had been laid over the list, inscribed with a message in big black letters--and affixed with the photo of Sarah, Frank, and little Grace that Harry had snapped earlier.

"ELF SARAH," read the message. "YOU ARE INVITED TO ATTEND GLOSSER'S CHRISTMAS EVE PARTY WITH SANTA CLAUS!"

Sarah stared for a long moment, stunned. Frank had caught her off-guard.

"Like it?" Frank rapped on the glass, and the faces of two male employees popped out from behind the green background curtains. Sarah recognized them but didn't know them by name. "The guys in the display department set it up for me." The guys behind the curtain waved, then popped back out of view. "I owe them big time, but it was worth it."

Sarah's head was spinning. She had hoped to keep pretending a while longer, but she was going to have to tell him. She was going to have to own up about Mike.

"Well?" Frank was grinning, oblivious. "What do you say?" He shook his Santa cap, swinging the white puff on the tip back and forth. "Will you go to Glosser's Christmas Eve party with Santa?"

Sarah's eyes were burning. Why couldn't he have left well enough alone?

"We'll have fun, I promise." Frank crossed his heart. "The most fun ever."

"I can't." Sarah backed away from the window. "I just *can't.*"

"Because you're engaged?"

Sarah's heart felt like it stopped. "You *knew?*"

Frank shrugged. "People talk, Sarah."

"You *knew,* and you kept...you did this *anyway?*" She flung up a hand at the window with the invitation inside.

"I *like* you. So sue me."

"But I'm *engaged.* I have a *fiancé.*"

"Who isn't here," said Frank. "Does he still make you happy, Sarah?"

"That doesn't have anything to do with this!"

Frank pressed his hands to his chest. "*I* make you happy, don't I?"

Sarah didn't answer.

"It's true and you know it," said Frank. "Just like I know that *you* make *me* happy."

"I can't do this." Sarah took another step away from him.

"You don't have to do anything," said Frank. "It's *your* life, isn't it?"

"No, no." Sarah turned away. She was going to miss

her bus. "I made a promise to him."

"Then why don't you wear your engagement ring?" asked Frank. "People talk about that, too, you know."

"Leave me alone!" With that, she hurried off across the snowy street, heading for the bus stop with tears streaming down her cheeks. "And find yourself another elf while you're at it!"

Frank didn't follow but called out after her. "The invitation stands! The party's tomorrow night!"

Sarah didn't answer him. She just kept running toward Main Street, waving frantically as the bus pulled up to the stop.

*****

That night, Sarah lay in bed and read the latest letter from Mike, the one about him not returning for at least six months. She read it again and again, crying harder each time.

"Honey?" Her mother knocked on the door of her bedroom. "Are you all right?"

"I'm fine," said Sarah.

She could hear Mom's hand on the doorknob. "You don't *sound* fine."

Sarah took a deep breath to steady her voice. "I am, thanks."

Mom hesitated. "Do you want to talk?"

Sarah was sure she already knew everything Mom

would say. "No, thanks. Goodnight."

Again, Mom hesitated. Then, the doorknob turned, and the tall, slender woman leaned into the room, her dark brown eyes full of concern. "Oh, honey. Is it Mike?"

Sarah wiped tears from her face. "I said I'm fine."

Mom walked all the way in and closed the door behind her. She was still wearing her housedress and Christmas apron after cleaning up the dinner dishes. "It's that letter he sent, isn't it?"

Sarah tossed the wrinkled and tear-stained letter on the bedside table. "Why can't things be simpler?" she said.

Mom sat on the foot of the bed. "What things?"

Sarah sighed and rubbed her eyes. "If Mike was here-- if my *fiancé* was here--I'd know just what to do."

Mom tipped her head to one side. "There's someone else, isn't there?"

Sarah's instinct was to deny it, but she nodded.

"I see." Mom crossed one leg over the other and tapped her bottom lip with a fingertip. "And you have feelings for him?"

Sarah felt the tears welling up, and a sob escaped her.

Mom nodded. Reaching up to pat her short brown hair, she stared at Sarah for a long moment. She looked like she was thinking something over, trying to decide whether or not to say it.

Then she said it. "I had a similar situation myself once, you know."

Suddenly, she had Sarah's undivided attention. It

33

wasn't at all what Sarah had expected to hear.

"That's right." Mom lowered her voice. "When your father was in Europe during the War, before we were married, there was...someone else."

"What?" Sarah sat up straight. *"Really?"*

"Shhh." Mom raised an index finger to her lips. "I don't want your father to know."

"Dad doesn't *know?"*

Mom's eyes widened. Emphatically, she struck the finger against her lips.

Chastened, Sarah lowered her voice. "Who was it?"

Mom shook her head. "What matters is, it was a similar situation. Your father and I got engaged in '43, and then he was gone for almost three years. And I...met someone."

"You mean...did you...?"

Mom slashed a hand through the air. "I wasn't that kind of girl. It was all very innocent." She shrugged. "If you don't count kissing."

Sarah leaned forward, seeing her mom with new eyes. "I just can't believe this. You never mentioned it before."

"It wasn't important to anyone else," said Mom. "But I'm not ashamed. Loneliness is a terrible thing, honey. And love..." She gave Sarah's ankle a squeeze. "Love is *rare* in this world."

Sarah sat back and looked over at the letter on the bedside table. "So you loved him?"

In reply, Mom gave her ankle another squeeze.

"But you married Dad anyway. You waited for him."

Mom nodded. "He's a good man. I did what I did."

"What about the other person?"

"Sometimes I wonder what happened to him." Mom sounded wistful. "But I don't suppose I'll ever know."

Sarah thought for a while, then flung her head back and blew out her breath. "I still don't know what to do."

"Whatever makes you happy," said Mom. "You're a 23-year-old woman, and your life is your own."

Again, Sarah was surprised by what Mom told her. She'd always thought of Mom as a straight-laced goody-two-shoes type...and now this. "Do you ever regret what you did or didn't do?"

Mom gave her ankle one more squeeze and got up from the bed. "Sometimes, yes. I wonder what life would be like if I'd chosen differently." Crossing the room, she reached for the doorknob. "But whatever you decide to do, remember that things have a way of working out." She opened the door and glanced back over her shoulder before leaving. "Especially at Christmastime."

*****

The next morning, Sarah was back to ringing up groceries. It was Christmas Eve day, and Glosser's grocery store was mobbed with folks stocking up for Christmas dinner--so the store manager had put a stop to Sarah's North Pole duty. He needed all hands on deck at the checkouts.

Which was probably just as well, after what had happened with Frank the day before. The display window he'd altered was back to normal...but Sarah was still sorting out her feelings. It might have been uncomfortable for her to go back to playing the role of Elf Sarah with Santa Frank for an entire shift.

So she really didn't mind being back at her checkout with Billy Cruikshank the bagger. It was actually a relief, a chance to forget about her problems and just throw herself into her work.

At least until a familiar hand shoved a familiar green cap in her face again.

"Put this on," said Frank. "And hurry."

For an instant, Sarah was furious. She spun, ready to give him a piece of her mind for interrupting her shift...and then quickly lost her rage.

She could tell from the look on his face that he wasn't goofing around, though he was wearing his Santa getup. Something was terribly wrong, and Frank was deeply upset.

"What's going on?" asked Sarah.

"We need to leave right now." Frank gave her the hat, then handed her the rest of her folded-up elf outfit. "It's important."

"But what--?"

Frank whipped around to jab a finger at Billy. "Get another cashier to cover for her. If anyone asks why, say it's an emergency."

Sarah was worried and confused at the same time. "What kind of emergency would I need an elf suit for?"

Billy scowled. "You don't give the orders around here, Frank Halloran."

"No, but David Glosser does, and he's the one telling you to get someone to cover for her!" Frank turned to Sarah and bobbed his head hard to one side, indicating that she should follow him. "Now let's go! We need to get to Lee Hospital right away!"

"Frank, wait!" Sarah ran after Frank as he charged toward the stairs. She was starting to panic a little. "Please tell me what's going on!"

Frank bounded up the stairs in a most un-Santa-like way, nearly bowling over shoppers on their way up or down. "It's Grace! The little girl from the photo! She's been in a car crash, and she's asking for us!"

*****

After changing into her elf costume in a ladies' restroom at the hospital, Sarah followed Frank to Grace's room. Over his shoulder, Frank lugged a full Santa sack, which a Glosser's co-worker had loaded and handed off on his way out of the store.

The good news, according to the duty nurse on the ward, was that the little girl's injuries weren't life-threatening or permanently debilitating. The bad news was, her Christmas had taken a turn for the worse.

"Ready?" Frank asked in a hushed voice in the hall outside Grace's door.

Sarah straightened her green felt cap. "That poor child." Her heart was racing. "Two broken legs and a broken arm..." She shook her head.

"And *we* are going to cheer her up." Frank shifted the sack on his shoulder and gave her a wink. "Are you okay with that? After last night?"

Sarah looked away, then returned her gaze to his face. Her mother's words came back to her. *Your life is your own.* "Yes." She nodded. "I'm okay."

Frank's bright green eyes held her, glittering. Slowly, a smile emerged beneath his bushy white beard. "Good. That's good."

He took a deep breath, then turned and marched through the doorway. "Ho ho ho! Merry Christmas Eve!"

As Sarah followed him in, she saw little Grace on the bed. Both legs and her right arm were bound in white plaster casts and suspended by traction apparatus mounted in the ceiling. Gauze was wrapped around her head and left eye, too, and there were bruises on her face and bare right arm. She looked like she ought to be utterly miserable--yet she still lit up at the sight of her visitors.

"Santa!" Grace's voice was weak and shaky, but her excitement still shone through. "And Elf Sarah! You came!"

"Of course we did!" Frank swung his sack onto a nearby chair. "A little bird told us we should stop by on the way to the North Pole!" He nodded at the girl's gray-haired grandmother, who sat in a chair beside the bed. Grandma nodded back.

"How are you feeling, Grace?" Sarah stepped up beside the bed and smiled down at the child.

"Worried about my mommy." Grace frowned. "But Grammy says she's okay."

"She got banged-up, too, but no broken bones," said Grammy. "Poor Grace got the worst of it, I'm afraid."

"Well, you're a brave and very talented little girl," said Frank. "Fixing those legs and that arm of yours like that."

"The *doctors* fixed those." Grace giggled.

"But I'll bet you helped them, didn't you?" Frank folded his arms over his chest and frowned. "Or were you *bad* again?"

Grace thought for a moment. "I cried. Does that count?"

"Of course not, honey." Sarah grinned and shook her head. "Especially after what you've been through."

"I *want* to cry now," said Grace. "'Cause Christmas is *ruined.*"

"Put those teardrops right back in your tummy!" said Frank. "Christmas is *never* ruined."

"But *look* at me! Doctor says I can't go home for Christmas! I won't be there when you bring my presents!"

"Oh, wait, that's right." Frank scowled as if deep in thought. "If only we had some way to get you those presents that didn't require you to be home."

When he flashed a wink at Sarah, she immediately caught on. "Santa?"

"Hmm." Frank folded his hands behind his back and paced across the room. "If only we could somehow bring them here to you."

Sarah cleared her throat. "I said, Santa!"

"But that's impossible, isn't it?" Frank paced to the doorway and leaned against the jamb, wagging his head. "It could never, ever *work*, could it?"

Eyes wide with feigned frustration, Sarah looked at Grace. "Doesn't he *remember*?" she said in a loud whisper.

Grace looked at the sack of gifts on the chair across the room and giggled.

"Oh, woe is me." Frank paced over to stand by the window, gazing out at the falling snow. "If only there was some way I could perform my Christmas duties for this sweet, sweet child!" He glanced over his shoulder at her and winced. "I mean, this *bad* child, but at least she's *honest* about it."

"Oh, San-ta!" Sarah tiptoed over to the chair with the sack of gifts and slid it toward it him. "I *have* something for you!"

"What shall I do?" Frank plunged his face into his red-mittened hands and pretended to weep. "How can I live this down?" Suddenly, he whirled and flung his arms out wide. "I'm not fit to be Santa Claus any..."

Just then, Sarah bumped the chair full of gifts into his legs. Again, she cleared her throat, louder than before.

"Oh, my." Frank pretended to notice the sack of gifts for the first time. "Look at that, won't you? What do you think is in that bag of mine, Grace?"

"*Presents!*" Grace laughed.

"I get so forgetful when I haven't had my milk and cookies!" Frank shook his head. "Thank you, dear Elf Sarah!"

"You're welcome, Santa." Sarah curtsied.

"A good elf is hard to find," said Frank. "I don't know what I'd do without her."

"You should give her a hug!" said Grace. "Elf Sarah needs a hug!"

Frank shrugged. "Well, she knows how much I appreciate her."

"Hug her, please?" said Grace. "For me?"

"Don't you want your presents first?" asked Frank.

"Hug her, Santa!"

Sarah looked at him, thought about it...then walked toward him with a kind of "let's humor the kid and get it over with" attitude.

This time, it was Frank's turn to clear his throat. "All right, then." He reached out and wrapped his arms around Sarah, as she did the same to him.

"And a kiss!" said Grace. "A hug *and* a kiss!"

Still in Frank's arms, Sarah leaned back and met his gaze. Smiling, she considered the promise in his eyes and what it might mean to her future.

If the future even mattered anymore. Maybe the

only thing that did matter was this moment in time, and this person who made her feel happy and less alone. Who accepted her and wanted her in his life as much as...

As much as she accepted and wanted him. And this kiss.

She closed her eyes and leaned toward him, and he did the same.

Their lips met, softly, through Santa's beard...and the feeling was electric in spite of the abundant whiskers. Her whole body tingled, and everything but him melted away around her.

It was the first time she'd kissed anyone since Mike had left for Korea, and it was magical. It was perfect.

Then, Grace cheered, and the moment was broken. Frank pulled away from her, smiling. She knew she was blushing as she smiled back at him.

"Oh no!" said Grace. "You forgot the mistle-toad!"

"No, he's right here." Frank tugged his Santa hat up and down and made *ribbet* noises. Grace giggled louder than ever. "Now how 'bout if we open those *presents*, huh?"

"Already got my present." Grace smiled contentedly.

"Tough beans." Frank slid the chair up beside the bed and opened the sack of gifts. "You got more where *that* came from, kid. Now repeat after me: Ho ho ho!"

"Ho ho ho!" said Grace.

Frank winked at Sarah, and she joined in, too. "Ho ho ho!"

"God bless us, every one!" said Frank as he pulled the

42

first gift out of the sack.

*****

Sarah and Frank stayed with Grace for hours, reading her stories and playing games and just talking. They stayed until she fell asleep, just as visiting hours were ending, and then they each kissed her forehead and left.

It was snowing hard when they stepped outside, big white flakes slashing down in the golden glow of the streetlights. All around, it was deeply quiet, amazingly peaceful for downtown Johnstown on a Thursday night, when the stores were usually open late and the streets full of people and cars.

As the two of them walked up Main Street, it seemed like they were the only people in the world. It felt to Sarah like a perfect moment, so magical that she couldn't resist when he reached to take her hand.

"Thank you," said Frank. "Thank you for coming along tonight."

"I wouldn't have missed it." Sarah walked close to him, enjoying the way his arm brushed against hers. "It was so wonderful, giving that poor girl a nice Christmas Eve."

"We did, didn't we?" Frank's smile was plain to see now that he'd taken off his Santa beard and stuffed it in his pocket. "We make a great team."

A car drifted past, laying tracks in the freshly fallen snow. For a second, Sarah thought about letting go of

Frank's hand--but then she caught herself and kept her hand right where it was.

"Can you think of a better way to spend Christmas Eve?" asked Frank. "Helping a little girl in the hospital?"

"I can't." Looking over at his smiling face, she had a rush of feeling for him--admiration and affection all at once. She was so proud of him for doing what he'd done and taking such obvious joy in it. He was a good person at heart...a good man.

"So much for the Christmas Eve party," said Frank. "But I don't mind, do you?"

Sarah shook her head. "This was more fun."

When they got to Central Park, they followed the snow-covered walk to the Christmas tree, its multi-colored lights glowing through the falling flakes. They stood there a while, side by side, gazing at the lights.

Then, he turned to her, his face blushing with reddish glow. "This is all I want for Christmas," he said softly. "All I could *ever* want."

When he leaned to kiss her, she didn't pull away.

*****

The next morning, Sarah woke bright and early and sailed across her bedroom, getting ready for Christmas Day. Frank had driven her home in his Chevy the night before, leaving her with one more kiss at the front door...and sweet dreams the whole night through.

As the sun streamed through her window that morning, Sarah realized she was happier than she'd been in a long time. The past two Christmases had been punishing, full of sadness because her fiancé was in Korea--but this one was full of hope. There was someone else who cared about her now, someone she cared about in return...and she was going to see him soon.

The night before, Frank had asked if he could come by around noon on Christmas Day, and she'd said yes. She hadn't told her parents yet, but she had a feeling it would work out fine. Dad might not be thrilled, but she knew Mom was on her side. Hopefully, Frank could even eat Christmas dinner with them.

The thought of it made her heart pound. She felt like she was finally moving forward after being frozen in place for so long.

The morning hours fell away like snowflakes as Frank's visit drew closer. After the family exchanged gifts around the tree, Sarah helped Mom with preparations for Christmas dinner. It was then she asked Mom if it was okay for Frank to join them...and Mom said yes.

Sarah was more worried about asking Dad, though, and put it off. She wasn't sure he'd appreciate the situation, as he'd once been in Mike's shoes himself, overseas with a fiancée at home during World War II.

Around noon, the doorbell rang, and Sarah knew it was too late. She would just have to wing it and hope for the best, hope her father would come to like Frank as much as she did.

"I'll get it!" She stopped peeling potatoes in the kitchen and dashed to the front door. One thing she didn't want was for Dad to get there first.

As the doorbell rang again, she straightened her hair, smoothed out her top, and took a deep breath. Smiling, she reached for the knob...so happy to be about to open the door and see *him* there. To know her Christmas was going to be *special* again.

She swung the door open, beaming expectantly. Her muscles tensed as she thought about holding him, kissing him...

And then, the world suddenly stopped turning.

Sarah's eyes locked on the face on the other side of the door, and she gasped. It wasn't Frank. It was the last person in the world she'd expected to see that day.

It was *Mike*.

"Merry Christmas, beautiful!" he said. "Miss me?"

*****

Sarah was in a state of shock. She just stood there in the doorway, gaping, speechless.

"Great surprise, huh?" Mike laughed amid the flurries glittering around him. He looked different from the last time she'd seen him, different even from the photos he'd sent from time to time——leaner, bonier, tougher. His dark eyes and big nose stood out more sharply from his knobby brows and sunken cheeks.

To Sarah, he was almost a stranger. "But your letter..."

Mike laughed again. "It was a setup! I've been discharged!"

"You mean...you're home?"

"Well, obviously! So is this the biggest surprise ever, or what?"

Sarah felt light-headed. She still couldn't believe this was happening. She still couldn't believe, after *everything*, that she'd opened the door to see *him* instead of...

Just then, a familiar blue Chevy pulled up at the curb. And Sarah's heart didn't just sink...it *nosedived*.

"So come on." Mike pointed at the sprig of mistletoe pinned to his olive drab cap. "Aren't you gonna give your fiancé a kiss?"

He spread his arms and grinned. Over his shoulder, Sarah saw Frank get out of the Chevy and walk toward them.

"Mike!" At that moment, Dad popped up behind her in the doorway. "You're back!" He was so excited, he pushed past Sarah to hug Mike himself.

Frank slowed down as he got closer, taking in the scene. Looking at Mike in his olive drab army fatigues and combat boots. Doing the math.

His eyes met Sarah's, and a world of understanding passed between them. She saw a flash of pain and disappointment, and she wanted to run to him. She wanted to comfort him, to take him in her arms as she'd intended and *care* for him. *Choose* him.

But she just stood there, frozen on the outside as she was tearing herself apart on the inside. She just *stood there...* thinking she needed more time, she needed to figure this out, she needed to do what was *right* for her.

It was one of those moments, she realized years later, that change a life forever.

As she watched, Frank gathered himself up and walked the rest of the way up the sidewalk. "Merry Christmas," he said brightly.

Everyone turned to look. "Who's this?" asked Dad.

Sarah cleared her throat. "This is Frank Halloran." She felt like she was speaking in a dream. "He works at Glosser's."

"As Santa Claus." Frank's smile was wide. Probably only Sarah could see how forced it was.

"Can we help you with something?" asked Dad.

Before Sarah could say a word, Frank answered. "I just stopped to give Sarah something." He dug in the pocket of his pea coat, came out with a closed fist. "Here you go." Leaning past Mike, he dropped the contents of his fist into Sarah's hand. "A little Christmas present for a co-worker."

He smiled then, only for her. For an instant, it was like before between them.

And then he whirled and hurried back to his car.

"What is it?" asked Mike.

Sarah opened her hand. A shiny penny rested head-up on her palm.

"A little money I owed you!" Frank said over his shoulder. "I always pay my debts, especially on Christmas!"

Sarah's eyes burned. Mike reached for the penny, and she snapped her hand closed around it.

"Merry Christmas!" shouted Frank. "God bless us every one!"

Sarah wanted to run after him. Almost did, for an instant...but then she didn't. She stayed instead.

As Frank drove off through the snow, the rest of his life somewhere in the distance.

*****

Johnstown, 2016

Sarah almost didn't get out of the car.

"Come on, Gram." Emma stood on the street with the car door open and reached in to help. "Jason and his grandfather are waiting."

Sarah frowned and shook her head. It had been 63 years since she'd last seen Frank Halloran, since he'd driven away from her house on Christmas Day. He'd moved away shortly thereafter and had never come back or reached out to her. The thought of seeing him again filled her with curiosity...but mostly panic.

"I shouldn't have let you talk me into this." She studiously kept her eyes from drifting toward the big Christmas tree in Central Park, just fifty feet away, which was where Frank was supposed to meet her. "I've changed my mind."

"Too late for that." Emma was determined to get her grandmother out of the car. She had high hopes that meeting Frank after so many years might restore Sarah's love of Christmas. Losing him, after all, was what had ruined the holiday for her in the first place.

"No." Clutching the silver locket at her throat, Sarah watched the reflected light from the tree flash and flicker on the windows of the car. "Not after the way things ended."

"He wants to see you, Gram." Emma smiled encouragingly. "He's okay with it. Otherwise, he wouldn't be here tonight."

"*He's* okay with it..." Sarah's voice trailed off. In 63 years, she had never forgiven herself for letting him go. She had never let herself celebrate Christmas.

Emma hunkered down and put a hand on her arm. "You have regrets, I get that. But you'll regret *this*, too, if you don't go to him now."

Sarah let out a long, shaky breath. She wished she could snap back to her usual sassy self with her take-no-crap attitude...but that part of her was switched off now. On the verge of reuniting with her long-lost love, all she felt was fear.

"Come on, Gram," said Emma. "He's a widower now. It's time for a second chance."

"What if you're wrong?" said Sarah. "What if it all goes south?"

Emma gave Sarah's arm a tug. She wanted this reunion for Sarah so much, wanted to bring some joy back into her life. "If things go south, I'll run you outta there like a bear out of a bee swarm."

Sarah stayed put another moment...then let Emma pull her out of the car. "The *second* they go south?"

"The *second*," said Emma, though she prayed she wouldn't have to keep her word.

"You better." Sarah snapped her fingers. "Or I will disinherit you like *that.*"

Emma laughed. "Now *there's* my Gram."

"Not for long if you don't get me outta there *pronto.*" Sarah glared as she pushed past her granddaughter and headed into the park.

*****

The crowd around the tree in Central Park was huge that night. After all, it was Christmas Eve.

Sarah moved slowly among the people, mindful of the coating of snow on the sidewalks. The big tree, like a beacon, guided her onward, its multicolored lights blinking and dancing amid the swirling flurries in the air.

Emma walked by her side, keeping one arm around her shoulders and holding on lightly to her elbow. She was a good girl, that Emma--even if she *was* pushing Sarah to do something she didn't want to do.

Just then, a little boy charged past, almost knocking

51

Sarah over. Another child followed, with a young mother bringing up the rear. "So sorry." She smiled apologetically on her way past.

It was amazing, what a difference that tree had made in such a short time. Funded by donations, spearheaded by a partnership of business people and volunteers, it had given new life to downtown Johnstown during the holidays. Practically deserted at night for many years, Central Park now reminded Sarah of the old days, when Glosser Bros. had still been packing them in.

It was appropriate, then, that as she approached the big tree, she suddenly saw Frank Halloran smiling back at her.

Even if his grandson, Jason, had not been standing nearby, Sarah would have recognized him instantly. Frank's hair was white instead of red, but his face was the same as ever. His body was as lean and athletic as before.

And somehow, as his green eyes met hers, the sparks were there between them again.

Sarah caught her breath. Her heart leaped in her chest like a bird taking flight.

Emma was saying something, but Sarah didn't hear a word of it. No one else mattered at that moment but him.

He called to her across the crowd, over the music from the flashing, blinking tree. "Elf Sarah!"

Tears ran freely from her eyes as she shuffled toward him. *To think,* she thought, *I almost didn't come here tonight.*

Frank didn't wait for her. Grinning, he rushed across the snowy walk and threw his arms around her, holding her tight against him.

*****

When Emma saw Sarah and Frank embrace, she flung up her hands in their wooly white gloves and clamped them over her mouth. She couldn't help herself from crying tears of pure joy to match those running down her grandmother's cheeks.

After all the wonderful things Sarah had done for her through the years, Emma was thrilled to give her this gift from the heart. She'd wanted to give her grandma back her love of Christmas, so she could enjoy it as much as Emma did...and now she had done just that. And more.

For there was *another* gift coming, a surprise.

"This is so great!" said Jason as he rushed over and threw an arm around her. "I think this is the happiest I've ever seen him!"

Sarah wiped tears from her face and nodded. "We did it! Oh my God, we did it!"

"Not like it took much work, though." Jason chuckled. "As soon as I mentioned her name, he was online checking plane fares! I think he was packing while we were still on the phone!"

"She was scared," said Emma. "But now look at them."

"And she doesn't know?" asked Jason. "About the surprise?"

Emma shook her head. "Why spoil it?" She grinned and turned to kiss him. "She should hear it straight from the horse's mouth."

*****

Sarah shut her eyes and savored every moment. How many times had she dreamed of this very thing happening over the past 63 years? How many times had she wished for this man to return to her?

Now there they were, a widow and a widower, basking in the light and magic of that special tree, across the street from the Glosser Bros. building where they'd first met in 1953.

"I told you I was a bad penny," he whispered in her ear. "Always turning up."

Sarah smiled with pure, boundless joy in his arms. She couldn't believe she'd been afraid.

"I'm so sorry," she said.

Leaning back, he shook his head. "Not me." Reaching out, he stroked the side of her face with his warm, rough hand. "Just *imagine* how good this *kiss* is going to be after all that time!"

As he leaned toward her, she saw Emma and Jason kissing out of the corner of her eye. She felt so overcome with emotion, she thought her heart might burst.

"By the way," said Frank. "I have a request."

"What's that?" asked Sarah, gazing lovingly into his

bright green eyes.

"Do you know anyone who could help me get settled?"

"Settled?"

"I'm moving back to town," said Frank. "Effective immediately. I'm sending for my things."

Sarah couldn't believe what she was hearing. "Really?" Her heart, which had already taken flight, was soaring into the loftiest heights now. "Immediately?"

Frank shrugged. "I've been considering it for a while, with my son and grandkids here. *Now* just seems...like the right time."

Sarah's smile widened. Her tears of joy quickened.

"So what do you say?" asked Frank. "Know anyone who could help..."

Sarah didn't let him finish his sentence.

As the tree played "I'll Be Home for Christmas," she lunged forward, pressing her lips against Frank's...and it was every bit as glorious as she'd imagined. She stopped thinking about fear and regret and second chances, stopped thinking about anywhere but *there*, anyone but *him*, and anything but that *kiss*.

And the penny he'd given her on that last day long ago, which she'd worn in a silver locket around her neck every day since, seemed to warm and glow like an ember between them, breathed back to life by the heat of their beating hearts.

Glosser's Christmas Photo Gallery

Photo courtesy Johnstown Area Heritage Association

Photo courtesy Ellen Ossip Sosinski

Photo by Kasey Hagens

Photo from Glosser Bros. Annual Report, Jan. 1978

Photo from Glosser Bros. Annual Report, Feb. 1975

A GLOSSER'S CHRISTMAS LOVE STORY

Photo from Glosser Bros. Annual Report, Jan. 1976

Photo by Philip Balko

Photo by Bob Hancock

Illustration by Ben Baldwin

ABOUT THE AUTHOR

Author and editor Robert Jeschonek grew up in Johnstown, Pennsylvania and spent many happy hours as a kid in the Glosser Bros. Department Store. Since then, he has gone on to write lots of books and stories, including *Long Live Glosser's, Penn Traffic Forever, Christmas at Glosser's, Easter at Glosser's, Halloweeen at Glosser's, Fear of Rain,* and *Death By Polka* (which are all set in and around Johnstown). He has written a lot of other cool stuff, too, including *Star Trek* and *Doctor Who* fiction and *Batman* comics. His young adult fantasy novel, *My Favorite Band Does Not Exist,* won a Forward National Literature Award and was named a top ten first novel for youth by *Booklist* magazine. His work has been published around the world in over a hundred books, e-books, and audio books. You can find out more about them at his website, www.thefictioneer.com, or by looking up his name on Facebook, Twitter, or Google. As you'll see, he's kind of crazy...in a *good* way.

CHRISTMAS AT GLOSSER'S

BY ROBERT JESCHONEK

Step back in time to Johnstown, Pennsylvania in 1975. Shoppers fill the downtown streets, bustling between the Glosser Bros. and Penn Traffic department stores... and one little boy runs through the crowd on a mission. Eleven-year-old Jack wants one thing for Christmas: to find out where his grandfather, Bub, runs off to every Christmas Eve. The trail leads him on a journey through Glosser Bros. at its most magical, but the magic takes an unexpected turn when he discovers Bub's secret. Before the night is over, Jack must take a stand in the name of Johnstown, a stand that could cost him everything...or bring him the greatest gift he can imagine.

AND NOW, A SPECIAL PREVIEW OF CHRISTMAS AT GLOSSER'S...

What happened in the secret sub-basement of Glosser's department store in Johnstown, Pennsylvania every Christmas Eve? Jack Shaffer found out in 1975, when he was eleven years old.

And then he found out what it felt like to die.

*****

"Where did you say you were going?" Mom stared at Jack through slitted eyes, holding one hand over the phone receiver in her grip.

"The library." Jack scrubbed his fingers through his short sandy hair in frustration. Mom had been talking on the phone and hadn't heard him the first two times he'd said it. "There's a book I need to get."

Mom waved him off. "Go on, then." She didn't ask if he was sure the library was open on Christmas Eve, didn't

1

tell him to be careful or hurry home. She wasn't always big on that sort of thing, since her latest boyfriend had moved out.

Jack pulled on his navy blue jacket over his red sweatshirt and bluejeans. "Seeya."

Mom didn't answer. Her hand was already off the receiver.

As Jack zipped up the jacket and marched toward the front door, he heard her talking excitedly into the phone again. "He'll definitely be at church tonight, Deb? You really think he'll like me?"

Scowling, Jack threw the door open and slammed it shut behind him. As he ran off down the street, all thoughts of Mom's dating life shot right out of him. He had bigger things on his mind, a mystery he needed to solve.

One involving the only man he truly cared about in the whole world.

*****

The door on the yellow-sided house two blocks from where Jack lived opened slowly, and a heavy tread came down on the front porch. As Jack watched from behind a tree on the other side of the street, a tall man with wavy silver hair stomped down the four steps from the porch to the sidewalk.

The man wore a dark gray jacket, zipped halfway up over a big pot belly. Under the jacket, he wore the same thing he wore every day--a crisp white button-down shirt and black tie. His trousers were black, too, and so were his immaculately shined Oxford shoes.

If Jack had called out to him at that moment--*Hey, Bub!*--the man would have grinned and waved him right over. Not only was he Jack's grandfather, Mom's dad, but he was Jack's biggest supporter, always there when he needed him.

Except for one night out of the year, that is. One night when he was nowhere to be found.

Christmas Eve.

Jack waited for Bub to get half a block down the street, then followed, taking care to stay far enough back that he wouldn't likely draw Bub's attention. Whenever he could, he lingered behind trees or lamp posts or parked cars, ever ready to duck down if needed...but Bub never looked back.

He just kept rambling down the street, eyes dead ahead, steering toward his mysterious errand.

Suddenly, a neighbor lady, Mrs. Williams, pushed open her car door in front of Jack. "Well, hello there, Jackie." She was in her eighties and stooped with arthritis but got around fine, even drove herself on errands. "Do you think you might help me with my groceries?"

Jack shook his head. "I'm sorry, Mrs. Williams, but I can't. I'm in a hurry."

"But it will just take a minute, Jackie."

"Next time, sorry." Jack's guts jittered when he looked up ahead where Bub should be. He was nowhere in sight.

Mrs. Williams was saying something, but Jack ran off without another word. No way was he going to wait another year to find out Bub's secret.

There was an intersection up ahead, and Jack charged toward it. Stopping on the corner, he looked right, then left, then stomped his foot angrily. He saw no sign of Bub in either direction.

Thinking fast, Jack sprinted forward, hoping for a glimpse of Bub down one of the cross-streets or alleys. He didn't spot him at the first street or even the second, but he caught a glimpse at the third--a flash of Bub's silver hair and gray jacket sliding past.

Jack gasped in relief and veered right down the side street. Reaching the end, he leaned out in time to see Bub disappear around a corner.

"Geez!" Jack panted as he darted after him. The old man was giving him a run for his money as he navigated the maze of the neighborhood in Dale Borough, not far from downtown Johnstown.

Peeking around the corner, Jack saw Bub continue straight ahead. He fell in behind him, keeping his distance as before.

And wondering what exactly Bub intended to do downtown, since that was where he was headed.

*****

What happens next? Find out in CHRISTMAS AT GLOSSER'S, on sale now!

ALSO BY ROBERT JESCHONEK

LONG LIVE GLOSSER'S
(A History of the Glosser Bros. Department Store)

CHRISTMAS AT GLOSSER'S

EASTER AT GLOSSER'S

HALLOWEEN AT GLOSSER'S

PENN TRAFFIC FOREVER
(A History of the Penn Traffic Department Store)

THE GLORY OF GABLE'S
(A History of Altoona's Gable's Department Store)

FEAR OF RAIN
(A Johnstown Flood Story)

THE MASKED FAMILY
(A Cambria County Story)

**NOW ON SALE AT AMAZON.COM,
BARNESANDNOBLE.COM,
OR BY REQUEST AT YOUR LOCAL BOOKSTORE**

Ask your bookseller to search by title at Amazon,
Ingram, or Baker and Taylor.

pie press publishing